Gabby Growing Up

BY AMY HEST

ILLUSTRATED BY AMY SCHWARTZ

SIMON & SCHUSTER BOOKS FOR YOUNG READERS

SIMON & SCHUSTER BOOKS FOR YOUNG READERS

An imprint of Simon & Schuster Children's Publishing Division

1230 Avenue of the Americas, New York, New York 10020

Text copyright © 1998 by Amy Hest

Illustrations copyright © 1998 by Amy Schwartz

All rights reserved including the right of reproduction in whole or in part in any form.

SIMON & SCHUSTER BOOKS FOR YOUNG READERS is a trademark of Simon & Schuster.

Book design by Lucille Chomowicz. The text for this book is set in Cochin.

The illustrations are rendered in gouache and pencil on Rives BFK paper.

Printed and bound in Hong Kong by South China Printing Co. (1988) Ltd..

First Edition 10 9 8 7 6 5 4 3 2 1

Library of Congress Cataloging-in-Publication Data

Hest, Amy. Gabby growing up / by Amy Hest; pictures by Amy Schwartz.

p. cm. Summary: Gabby has knitted mittens to give her grandfather for his birthday,

and on their way to meet him, Gabby gets a new haircut and her mother gets a surprise.

ISBN 0-689-80573-X

[1. Grandfathers—Fiction. 2. Mothers and daughters—Fiction. 3. Birthdays—Fiction.]

I. Schwartz, Amy, ill. II. Title. PZ7.H4375Gab 1998 [E]—dc21 96-53145

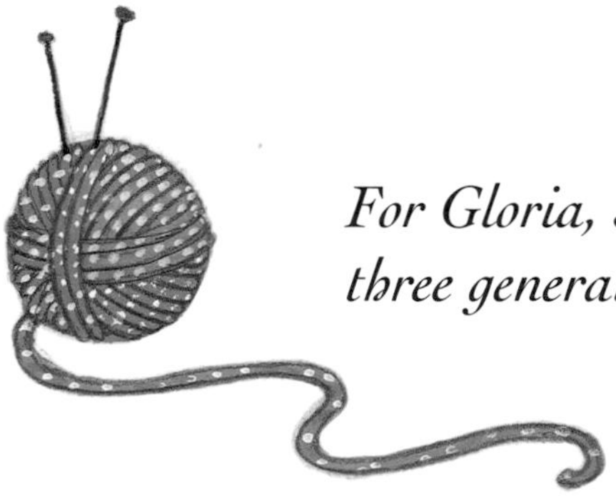

For Gloria, Jessica, and Remy—
three generations

—A. H.

To Jane

—A. S.

On the morning of Grampa's birthday, Gabby got up before the sun to put the finishing touches on his present. She reached under the bed for her bag of yarn and those long, poking needles.

Hello, beauties! Gabby couldn't wait to show Grampa his brand-new mittens. She made them herself. With just a little help from Mama.

Gabby looped and pulled. Stitch after stitch. She looped and pulled and stopped. Then she started all over. Gabby looped and pulled and sighed. Knitting was not easy.

Soon it was time to go to the city. Mama read from her list, making check marks with a pencil. THINGS TO DO IN THE CITY. "First, there's your haircut, Gabrielle. Just a trim," she said, "like always (check). Number two is shopping (check). And then . . ."

"You forgot to say 'Grampa,'" Gabby interrupted.

"Grampa comes *after* lunch."

"That's too many hours," mumbled Gabby. "It's hard to wait."

Mama was holding a pink-and-white-striped box with a string for a handle. There must be a hat inside. Mama loved hats and bought one every week or month. But most of the hats went right back to Saks Fifth Avenue, after Mama concluded they were too big or small, too plain or fussy, or just too something.

"What if Grampa doesn't like mittens?" Gabby said. "I should have made a muffler."

"Grampa likes mittens," Mama said. "Everyone likes mittens."

"What if he hates orange?" Gabby wrinkled her nose. "I should have made purple."

"Grampa is a big fan of orange," Mama said.

"My mittens have too many crooked stitches." Gabby sighed. "And bumps in both thumbs!"

Mama shook her head. "So many worries for such a small girl."

The Silver Express chugged into the station. Gabby found a
seat near the window so she could watch the snowy trees pass by.
Across the aisle sat another girl, old enough to be a high school
girl. The girl crossed her legs. Gabby crossed hers. The girl
opened a book on her lap. Gabby opened hers, too.

When the girl took off her hat and combed her hair with a polka-dot comb, Gabby gasped, "Mama, look! Her hair is so short, and I love the way her ears peek out!"

"That's a perky little haircut," Mama agreed.

"Perky hair. Short hair, short-to-your-ears-hair," Gabby sang to herself.

After the train, the uptown bus. Then one of Mama's brisk city walks all the way to King's, which smelled more like a perfume factory than a department store. Gabby loved clicking her shoes on the old wood floor.

Leo's Barber Shop was at the top of the escalator. On the way up Mama said, "We'll tell Leo the usual—one inch, please. Off with the raggedy ends!"

Gabby sucked in her breath. "This time," she announced, "I want short hair. Really short, to my ears."

"To your ears?" Mama squeaked.

"I'm tired of braids, tired of tangles, and these rubber bands pull. Long hair is hateful to wash. The shampoo won't come out, and you rub my head too hard with the towel, and it hurts!" Gabby pushed her lower lip out. "I want short hair."

Mama held her forehead. "Braids suit you," she said.

"Braids used to suit me"—Gabby climbed into Leo's big chair—"but not anymore. I want short hair."

Mama's foot tapped the floor. "You'll look too grown-up, Gabrielle." *Tap, tap. Tap-a-tap-tap.*

"But I *am* growing up," Gabby pointed out.

Leo was rubbing his bushy eyebrows. "Hair does grow," he said. "It always grows back." He draped a towel all around Gabby, then a turquoise-colored apron.

Mama backed into a barber's chair. "Cut away if you must"—her shoes slipped to the floor—"and just let me know when it's over."

Leo snipped. He sang tra-la-la. Gabby tried not to wriggle, but she was hot. Leo snipped and snipped. Gabby tried not to squirm, but she was very itchy. She tried not to look down, but—oh, no—her braids were on the floor!

When it was over, Gabby's hair was short. Really short, to her ears.

"Beautiful!" cried Leo.

"I don't look like me," Gabby whispered.

"It will take getting used to." Mama held Gabby's chin. She tilted her head one way, then the other.

"My ears stick out at the bottom," Gabby said. "Do they stick out too much, Mama?"

"I don't think so," Mama said.

"Fantastic!" Leo cried.

"I look older." Gabby frowned. "Do I look too old, Mama?"

"Maybe just a little." Mama's lips curled up, but not very much. "On the other hand, Gabrielle, you do look rather perky."

"Charming!" Leo cried. "Yes?"

Gabby looked and looked in the mirror. Then she said, "Let's ask Grampa."

Gabby's favorite restaurant had revolving doors and curvy counters and tall stools that spun around. The waitresses never smiled, but they brought the hot dogs fast.

"Now is it time for Grampa?" Gabby patted her short hair.

"Soon," Mama said.

"Will Grampa like my haircut?" Gabby curled her short hair with two fingers.

"I hope so," Mama said.

"What if he just pretends?"

"Grampa does not pretend," Mama said.

"What about the mittens?" Gabby asked. "What if he doesn't like those?"

"But you made them yourself, Gabrielle! Grampa will be thrilled!"

"What if he just pretends?"

Mama smoothed Gabby's cheek, then she kissed it.

It was finally time to find Grampa. "Imagine a park smack in the middle of the city," Gabby sang, "and a skating rink smack in the middle of that!" She skipped ahead on winding paths.

Mama tried keeping up, but high heels were not good for running, and that hatbox kept bumping her knee.

"I don't see Grampa, Mama! What if he forgets?"

"Grampa, forget?" Mama laughed. "I bet he's on the ice already." She checked her list. "Remember, mittens *after* skating. It's fun to save surprises for the end."

"Well, it's no fun to wait," Gabby said, exchanging her shoes for size-two skates at the skate shop.

Gabby leaned on Mama as they inched toward the bright winter sunshine and the shimmery ice rink.

"Hello! Hello!" Grampa skated over. He stopped with a flourish and hugged them both in woolly arms. He wore the same green sweater as always, but today there were other layers, too, in rainbow colors.

"Happy birthday, Grampa!"

"Having a lovely day, Pop?"

Grampa winked. Then he bowed to Gabby and led her onto the ice.

"I have a present for you," Gabby told Grampa the minute Mama left to do her city shopping.

"When do I get to see it?"

"Soon, Grampa. Mama says we have to wait."

Gabby wished she could dance the way Grampa danced on ice. Grampa could dip and spin. He could even skate backwards. And he never once fell down.

"Something is different about you," Grampa said.

"You guess!" Gabby tried a twirl, but only got halfway.

"New hat?"

Gabby shook her head.

"Did you grow new freckles?"

Gabby shook her head again.

"No more braids!"

"It is *very* short," Gabby said in her worried voice, "and my ears stick out."

"I see that." Grampa nodded.

Gabby licked her lips. "Do you like it?" she asked. "Do you like it just a little?"

"Hmmmm." Grampa took a good, hard look. "I certainly liked those braids, Gabrielle." He rubbed his chin. "On the other hand, I think . . . well . . . I think your haircut is . . . splendid. Really, really fine."

"I look more grown-up," Gabby pointed out.

"Maybe a little," Grampa said. "But what's the rush to be grown-up?"

"That's just what Mama says."

Grampa sniffed. "Your mother couldn't *wait* to look grown-up when she was your age!"

"Did she cut her braids, too?"

"Did she ever!" Grampa shook his head. "Cut them *herself*, right over the kitchen sink!"

"Mama did *that*?" Gabby shrieked.

"And that was just for starters. Next, she wanted shoes without laces . . . pink lipstick . . . before I knew it, she was going to dances with boys and . . ."

"Grampa, stop!" Gabby cried. "I want to do my growing up slowly."

"I'm with you," Grampa said. "Gabby growing up," he added, "one day at a time."

Gabby and Grampa warmed their hands on mugs filled high with cocoa.

"Your birthday present is right here in my pocket. I made it myself. How about a little peek," Gabby whispered, "while we wait for Mama?"

Grampa drummed his fingers on his knees. "I suppose one tiny little peek wouldn't hurt."

They huddled over the package. Gabby made a small tear at one corner. Grampa bent closer. She made another tear, at another corner.

"Mittens!" Gabby cried. "Do you like them, Grampa, do you?"

"Ahem!" Mama made a coughing sound behind them. "You two, always up to something . . . but you're not the only ones!" She turned on her heel and marched into the lodge. Gabby and Grampa followed.

Suddenly the lights went out . . . then little flicking lights snapped on . . . and there was singing. All around were skaters and nonskaters, and they were singing "Happy Birthday" to Grampa! And right in the middle was Mama, holding a cake with candles for Grampa to blow out. When he did, everyone cheered.

Mama cut the cake, and there was plenty to go around.

"What a wonderful surprise!" Grampa said.

"How did you do it, Mama?" Gabby asked.

Mama laughed. She pointed to the pink-and-white-striped box. "I bet you thought there was a hat inside!"

After the cake, Grampa put on his brand-new mittens. "I love them," he announced. "Such a splendid shade of orange!"

"They're lumpy in spots," Gabby said in her quiet, worried voice, "and some stitches are crooked, and . . ."

"And you made them yourself, just for me." Grampa kissed the tip of her nose. He hugged Mama tight.

"Happy birthday, Pop." Mama dabbed at her eyes with a hankie.

Then Gabby and Grampa went out on the ice, and they skated around and around until the music stopped.